ANDREW'S AMAZING MONSTERS

by Kathryn Hook Berlan
illustrated by Maxie Chambliss

ATHENEUM 1993 NEW YORK

Maxwell Macmillan Canada
TORONTO
Maxwell Macmillan International
NEW YORK   OXFORD   SINGAPORE   SYDNEY

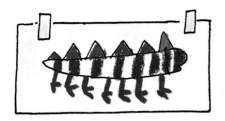

Atheneum   Maxwell Macmillan Canada, Inc.
Macmillan Publishing Company   1200 Eglinton Avenue East
866 Third Avenue   Suite 200
New York, NY 10022   Don Mills, Ontario M3C 3N1

Macmillan Publishing Company is part of
the Maxwell Communication Group of Companies.

First edition
Printed in Singapore
10 9 8 7 6 5 4 3 2 1
The text of this book is set in 16 point Palatino.
The illustrations are rendered in watercolors.

Library of Congress Cataloging-in-Publication Data
Berlan, Kathryn Hook.
Andrew's amazing monsters / by Kathryn Hook Berlan; illustrated
by Maxie Chambliss. —1st ed.
p.   cm.
Summary: The monster drawings on Andrew's walls come to life and
give him a party.
ISBN 0-689-31739-5
[1. Monsters—Fiction.   2. Drawing—Fiction.   3. Parties—
Fiction.]   I. Chambliss, Maxie, ill.   II. Title.
PZ7.B45325An 1993
[E]—dc20   91-39131

Andrew loved monsters.
 He watched monster movies and bought
monster toys.

He even painted monsters on his shirts and sheets,
until his mother took his paints away.

After that his father brought home a big package
of white paper and a box of crayons.

Andrew's father said firmly, "These are magic
monster crayons, but they *only* work on paper."

Andrew loved his magic monster crayons!
Every day he drew monsters.
Big monsters…and little monsters.

Tall, skinny monsters
...and short, fat monsters.
Green, scaly monsters
...and slimy yellow monsters.

The more monsters Andrew drew,
the more amazing they looked.
Andrew drew striped monsters,
…plaid monsters,
…rainbow monsters,

...monsters with thirty-three toes
with terrible claws,
...monsters with nine heads filled
with needle-sharp teeth,
...monsters with great flapping wings
and fiery breath.

Andrew covered his walls with monster pictures.
His monsters looked so real they seemed to wiggle
and roll their eyes.

Andrew would smile and say, "Sit still, monsters."

One night Andrew drew party hats and horns for all of his monsters.

His monsters seemed to shuffle their feet and wag their tails.

Sighing, Andrew said, "I wish we could have a real party."

When he was climbing into bed, Andrew heard his monsters giggling and whispering.

Andrew shushed them and said, "Go to sleep, monsters!"

And everything was quiet.

Later Andrew was awakened by more whispering
and rustling in the dark. He clicked on his flashlight
and looked around the room. His monsters were
gone! Only the empty papers hung on the wall.

Andrew searched his room. He looked in his closet…under his bed…and behind his dresser. He couldn't find the monsters anywhere.

Climbing up on his bed, Andrew frowned and called, "Where are you hiding, monsters?"

But the monsters didn't answer.

Andrew switched off the light and peered into the blackness.

His door creeeeeeeeaked open.

Something shuffled and snuffled and gruffled out the door.

Something flopped and hopped and clopped down the hall.

Something thumped and bumped and jumped up the attic stairs.

Something giggled and groaned and wiggled and moaned in the attic.

Andrew eased off the bed and flicked on his
flashlight.
    He tip-tiptoed down the hall.

He slip-slip-slipped up the stairs.

At the top of the stairs, Andrew heard hissing and shushing behind the attic door.

Andrew threw open the door.

His monsters filled the room, howling and hooting, writhing and wriggling, chortling and cheering. They shouted:

"Surprise, Andrew!"

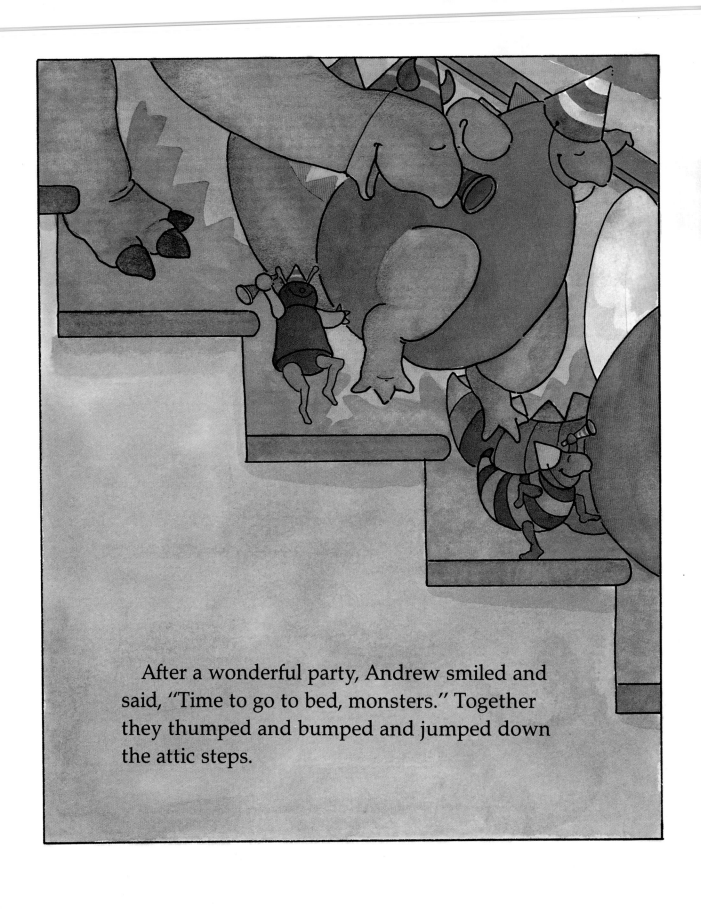

After a wonderful party, Andrew smiled and said, "Time to go to bed, monsters." Together they thumped and bumped and jumped down the attic steps.

They flopped and hopped and clopped along the hall.

They shuffled and snuffled and gruffled into Andrew's room.

Andrew's monsters hurried and flurried and
scurried onto their papers as Andrew climbed into
his warm, cozy bed.

Andrew smiled and said, "Go to sleep, monsters."
…And this time they all did.